QUARRY STORY

⊶ A History of ⊷

THE BROWNSTONE QUARRIES OF PORTLAND, CT

WRITTEN AND ILLUSTRATED BY
Kearen Enright

ISBN: 1460977920
ISBN-13: 9781460977927

QUARRY STORY

⊰⊱ *A History of* ⊰⊱

THE BROWNSTONE QUARRIES OF PORTLAND, CT

WRITTEN AND ILLUSTRATED BY
Kearen Enright

*This book is dedicated to
the Brownstone Quarry Quorum
for their vision of such a beautiful place.*

Thank you to my wonderful family and friends
for putting up with all my crazy quirks. Thank you
to Paul and Dana for pushing with just enough
sarcasm to inspire me. Thank you to Colleen Brede,
Bob McDougall, Alison Guinness, Nancy Smith,
and Jeanne Dilworth for their help. And,
a special thank you to Alice Schumacher
for asking me if I would be interested in writing
a book about the Brownstone Quarries.

To Freddy & Tom -
Come back & see us again
Enjoy -

"Are you really 300 years old, Grandpa John?"

I could see his open newspaper shake, and he grumbled under his breath, trying very hard to sound grumpy. He tried that a lot, but he never succeeded.

"Mama, is Grandpa John really 300 years old?"

"Well, Olivia …if Grandpa says he's 300, it must be true," she said as she winked at me and flipped my bacon in the sizzling pan.

"After breakfast do you want to go for a walk with me, Liv?" Grandpa asked.

"Can we go down to the quarry?"

"That is your favorite walk, isn't it?" He said this as more of a statement than a question. Anyone who knew me knew that I loved to go down by the quarry.

"You stay away from the edge! You hear me, young lady?" My mother scolded.

"I know Mama! I'm careful. I'm always careful!" I really always was. I had heard many stories of kids falling into the water off the cliffs. I wasn't about to have that happen to me!

1

I couldn't eat my breakfast fast enough, but I think Grandpa John had an extra cup of coffee just to torture me. When he was done, I put on my sneakers and a jacket and we were on our way. We walked down to Main Street, past the pavilion that covers a large old wooden piece of equipment that looks like a cart.

"This old machine is called an arch, or a sling," Grandpa explained. "It was used to help oxen lift stone in the quarries a long time ago." I had always wondered what that thing was, and Grandpa John knew everything. Then, just before we got to the big bridge, we turned toward the Connecticut River. Grandpa smiled down to me and he put out his hand for mine. His hands seemed enormous, and they were always nice and warm. His fingers were knobby and wrinkled. "Your hands look like an old tree trunk, Grandpa."

"Well, now, that's because I am part oak tree, Olivia. That is how I got to be so old," he said, giving me a wink that looked very much like the one Mama had given me earlier. Suddenly, Mama and Grandpa looked very much alike to me.

We made our way down the little street. As we walked, a chipmunk darted from underneath a stone to a tree just ahead of us. I ran to try to get a better look at it.

"He went into a hole in this tree!" I hollered back to Grandpa John.

"Ah, that little guy is living in my cousin," he said with a laugh.

"Oh Grandpa, you are teasing me again!" I was sure of it this time.

4

Grandpa's eyes twinkled and he tried not to laugh. "This is...Oliver Oak. You were named after him."

"I was named after a TREE?" I gasped. "Well, at least it's my favorite one."

This really was my favorite tree and my favorite spot to go with Grandpa. From here we could see cliffs, the beautiful quarry, and the river below us. Grandpa seemed to like my answer.

"A long time ago, this old tree was planted here by a little boy. How old are you?"

"Nine on April 9th," I told him.

"What a coincidence! A little boy who was nine years old planted this tree, before there was even a town here, back before there was a quarry. The boy planted the tree the day he and his family moved from across the river. Would you like me to tell you about this old quarry, Olivia?"

Grandpa John was a great story teller and the quarry was my favorite place, so that was an easy one. "Yes!"

"Well okay then…" he began, as we walked down the hill. "The boy's father was James Stancliff, a stonecutter from England. Mr. Stancliff noticed the reddish brown stone that hung over the river. He moved his family here, and used the stone to make grave markers to sell.

"Mr. Stancliff and his family were the first to settle in this area and he started the quarrying.

"That little boy grew up and moved away, but the tree grew too. It was more than 100 years after the boy planted Oliver before quarrying became a big business, but by then everyone had noticed the wonderful quality of the stone here."

As Grandpa John was telling his story, we again started walking down the street toward the river. Just the street and a small bit of land divided the river from the quarry at the bottom of the hill.

"Now that we are so close to the river, you can see how the men were able to get the stone onto the big ships. Gildersleeve Ship Construction Company was right over there," Grandpa said as he pointed up river.

"One of our schools is named Gildersleeve, Grandpa John!" I said excitedly. "Oh…and another is named Brownstone!" Suddenly, it seemed to me that everything in town was connected to my favorite spot.

Grandpa smiled knowingly down to me. "New York City was growing very quickly and everyone wanted beautiful, carved stone for their new buildings. The stone here was perfect. This created a huge demand for brownstone, and the pressure to move all that brownstone created the need for ships so the stone could be taken as far as San Francisco and even Europe. The stone from this quarry was used in many cities, but almost all of the brownstone in New York City came from our little town of Portland.

"Because of quarrying and shipbuilding, this area grew very fast. Portland separated from Middletown and became a town of its own. It was named after a famous quarry in England.

The need for workers brought groups from many different countries to live here. People came from Sweden, Ireland, and even Italy. The quarrying business became so huge that more than 1,500 men worked at the Brownstone Quarries at one time."

"Wow Grandpa! That is a lot!"

"Yes, Olivia, it was a lot. Quarrying was hard work, though. The men worked more than 10 hours a day when it was warm outside, but they had no work in the winter months. The stone cracks if it is taken out of the ground wet and it freezes, so they could quarry only when it wasn't too cold."

"Is that how we got this hole, by digging up all the stone?" I asked. It was the first time I noticed that the quarry was really a huge hole. The steep cliff walls were where the stone had been cut away. At the bottom was a beautiful lake.

"Yes, smart girl! As the workers took more and more stone, they dug deeper and deeper into the land. In the early days of the quarry, the rock was dragged out by oxen and horses. As the quarry became deeper, the animals would be led into large boxes and swung out over the pit to be lowered as much as 150 feet with big wooden rigs called derricks and cranes."

"Oh Grandpa, those poor animals must have been so scared!" I couldn't help shouting.

He laughed aloud. He knew I was kind of afraid of heights. "Sometimes children would even be allowed to ride down in buckets to deliver lunch to their fathers."

I tried to look out over the edge of the cliff. "I wouldn't like that! I would be afraid. Mama would be M- A- D!" Just the thought of how mad she'd be made me squirm.

"Eventually, a drawbridge was built, linking the quarry to the railroad. A few years later, a track was built around the quarry, so they didn't have to use the oxen anymore."

"Well, that's good." I didn't like the idea of the oxen being lowered down in boxes and working so hard.

Grandpa John continued: "Over time, steel and concrete were introduced. These were stronger, easier to use, and less expensive, so people started to make big, tall sky scrapers. They used less and less brownstone.

"Then, in 1936, there was a huge flood. The water from the Connecticut River ran right into the quarry, filling it up. Most of the equipment was destroyed. The owner tried to drain the water, but just two years later there was a horrible hurricane, and the quarries flooded again. Since people were not using as much brownstone for building anymore, it didn't make sense to keep trying to drain the water.

This time the quarry was left abandoned. Vines grew everywhere, and the only people that came here were teenagers, swimming and diving into the dangerous waters, and people dumping junk and stolen cars."

I thought about that and it made me sad. "Oh, I bet that was hard for Oliver Oak," I said. I was pretty proud of myself for adding to Grandpa's story.

Grandpa smiled and continued. "There was one time when there was a long drought and the town's reservoir dried up. Water was pumped out of the quarry and supplied the townspeople with water for 45 days. For the most part, however, the quarry was abandoned for almost 50 years."

We walked around to the other side of the quarry. It was much busier. There were big trucks and machines everywhere, and big pieces of brownstone all around. We met a friend of Grandpa's. "Olivia, this man owns this quarry business," Grandpa said as he introduced us. I was absolutely amazed.

"I didn't know there was still quarrying now," I blurted out. Then I felt that perhaps I should not have said that. Grandpa's friend was very nice, though, and began to show us what he was working on.

"I started this small-scale quarrying operation in the 1990's," he told us. "Most of the work we do now is fixing old buildings."

"They use modern techniques and machinery," Grandpa said with a wink. "No oxen here." Grandpa's friend smiled too, I guessed he understood the joke.

"Olivia, would you like to see a dinosaur footprint?" The man asked.

I had seen fossils and footprints in museums, but never when I was just out for a walk with my Grandpa.

"Sure!"

We walked around a pile of big blocks of stone that had been cut from the quarry. Some looked as if they were going to be big benches, others were huge slabs. Then he stopped and climbed onto one of the biggest ones of all. There, in the middle of it, was a great big dinosaur print! "COOL!"

Grandpa's friend had such a nice friendly face. "I think its cool too, Olivia," he said. "When the sand and silt was washing down from high lands and settling in this area, layer upon layer to form rock, dinosaurs were walking around right here!"

It suddenly made me think of what the land was like millions of years ago, in our little town of Portland (well, before it was our little town).

We said goodbye to Grandpa's friend and then walked across the street to the Portland Riverfront Park. It was peaceful and very quiet. We were right next to the river with a lot of big trees all around us. By the water there were benches made of brownstone slabs like the ones we had just seen being cut. Some of the benches even had nice markers on them saying that they were placed there to remember someone special.

We sat on one of the benches, quietly watching the river rush by. I felt different about the Connecticut River, Portland, and about the quarry than I had this morning. This had been my favorite walk before, but now it seemed so much more special.

"Well, I think we had better head back home or your Mom will think that we have fallen in," Grandpa finally said.

I was sure that he was right; my mother did worry a lot. So we started our walk back.

"When did they put in the zip lines, slides, and the other fun stuff, Grandpa?" I asked. Now summer could not come quickly enough for me.

"Well, the most wonderful thing happened. There was a small group of townspeople who were sad that the quarry was such a mess. They wanted to see something nice done with it. They pulled the old cars and garbage out of the water and worked very, very hard to clean up the land. Then, in the year 2000, they were even able to get the quarry declared a National Historic Landmark.

"The group talked to three brothers who had the idea of starting the Discovery and Exploration Park. The brothers were the ones who set up the floats, rock climbing, picnic areas, and all of the park's attractions. It was a great idea because it gets people using the quarry but not hurting it. Now there is a place for people to swim, picnic, kayak, scuba dive, and have all sorts of fun and adventures!" As he said this, we stopped back where we had started, at our favorite tree, and looked across the quarry. "People are able to enjoy the beauty of these quarries, the way that Oliver always has."

I thought about the kids who used to take lunches down to their fathers in the quarry. I wanted to be brave too. "Grandpa, when the Exploration Park is open, do you think I could try one of those zip lines?"

Grandpa John gave me his biggest smile. "You've got plenty of oak in you; you can do anything!" he said. I wasn't quite as certain as he was, but I couldn't help laughing. "Oliver told me that sometimes he even sees kids that remind him of that Stancliff boy from all those years ago."

QUARRY FACTS:

- Brownstone is naturally broken into blocks, with cracks called keys and joints. Keys are cracks that run side to side, created as different layers of rocks formed from silt and sand. Joints are cracks that go up and down, and are created by shifts in the land. Early settlers of the area would collect natural blocks of brownstone for foundations, chimneys, steps, and hearthstones.

- Brownstone was often called "freestone." Not because the people could gather the stone without a charge, but because the stone could be taken from the land often already in blocks, not connected.

- Portland's town emblem features oxen pulling with a "sling" or "arch". One remains preserved under the Arch Pavilion on Main Street. It is the oldest artifact of Portland's quarrying history.

- 1665 - Middletown realized the value of its natural resource and began to charge people outside Middletown for the brownstone.

- 1690 -James Stancliff, an English stonecutter, moved his family across the Connecticut River. He was granted the right to use the stone for business in exchange for making the town's buildings chimneys. The Stancliffs were the first settlers of what would become Portland, and first to quarry brownstone.

- 1711 - The first school was built in the area, which was then still part of Middletown, Connecticut.

- 1767- Middletown, East of the river, becomes the town of Chatham.

- 1783 – The firm of Hurburt and Roberts purchases land for quarrying, which later became the Brainerd Quarry.

- 1788 - Shaler and Hale Company started on the land that had been owned by Stancliff. It was a substantial quarrying business.

- 1812 – Erastus and Silas Brainerd purchase the Brownstone Quarry from Hurburt and Roberts.

- 1819 - Patten and Russel start quarrying next to the Shaler and Hall quarry.

- 1828 – Sylvester Gildersleeve consolidated many shipyards to establish S. Gildersleeve and Sons, which built more than 350 ships.

- 1841 - Chatham itself split up and the area became a town in its own right. The people had a little trouble deciding on a name. On June 1st, the people called the town Middlesex, on June 2nd they changed it to Conway, and then on June 4th they decided to name it Portland, after Portland, England, which was famous for its quarries.

- From 1850 to 1880 the population of Portland almost doubled. At the height of the industry, there were three commercial brownstone quarries in Portland. The quarrying business became so successful that by 1880 more than 1,500 men worked at the Portland quarries, and 25 ships were used to transport the stone all over the country.

- The popularity of brownstone was increasing as ornately carved buildings called "Gothic Revival" or "Romantic" styles became the trend. The population growth in New York City created a great demand for Portland's stone. The stone was shipped as far as San Francisco and was used in many cities, but it is estimated that 90% of the brownstone in New York City came from the little town of Portland.

- The demand for quarry workers brought many people from all over the world to live here. First Englishmen and Scotsmen, and then many people from Ireland and Sweden, and later still groups from Italy and Poland came to work in the quarries.

- 1861 – 1865 Civil War: 10% of the men from Portland went to fight.

- 1872 – A truss-type drawbridge built. This connected the quarries to the railroad.

- 1822 – 1849 – Middletown was given money from the quarry to help build Wesleyan University.

- 1884 - A railroad was built around the quarries, eliminating the need for many of the oxen.

- 1896 – Highway Bridge was built. Now trolley cars could travel from Portland to Middletown. Within 20 years, however, it was out of date. Cars had to wait every time a tall boat went up or down the river.